"I tell you what, you stay right here!"
FRONTISPIECE. *See page 39.*

CHILDREN'S THRIFT CLASSICS

The Adventures of Danny Meadow Mouse

THORNTON W. BURGESS

Original Illustrations by Harrison Cady
Adapted by Thea Kliros

PUBLISHED IN ASSOCIATION WITH THE
THORNTON W. BURGESS MUSEUM AND THE
GREEN BRIAR NATURE CENTER, SANDWICH, MASSACHUSETTS,
BY
DOVER PUBLICATIONS, INC., NEW YORK

DOVER CHILDREN'S THRIFT CLASSICS
EDITOR: PHILIP SMITH

This Dover edition, first published in 1993 in association with the Thornton W. Burgess Museum and the Green Briar Nature Center, Sandwich, Massachusetts, who have provided a new introduction, is an unabridged republication of the work first published by Little, Brown, and Company, Boston, in 1915. The original halftone illustrations by Harrison Cady have been adapted in line format by Thea Kliros for this edition.

Library of Congress Cataloging-in-Publication Data

Burgess, Thornton W. (Thornton Waldo), 1874–1965.
The adventures of Danny Meadow Mouse / Thornton W. Burgess ; original illustrations by Harrison Cady adapted by Thea Kliros. — Dover ed.
     p.   cm.
"Published in association with the Thornton W. Burgess Museum and the Green Briar Nature Center, Sandwich, Massachusetts."
Reprint. Originally published: Boston : Little, Brown, 1915. With a new introd.
Summary: Danny Meadow Mouse, a timid but quick vole, plays hide-and-seek with his foe Reddy Fox and has other adventures with the animals of the Green Meadows.
ISBN-13: 978-0-486-27565-9
ISBN-10: 0-486-27565-5
[1. Voles—Fiction.   2. Animals—Fiction.]   I. Cady, Harrison, 1877–
, ill.   II. Kliros, Thea, ill.   III. Title.
PZ7.B917Abd   1993
[Fic]—dc20   92–36950
                                                                    CIP
                                                                    AC

Manufactured in the United States by Courier Corporation
27565512
www.doverpublications.com

Introduction to the Dover Edition

LITTLE DANNY MEADOW MOUSE was timid. All the animals of the Green Meadows agreed on that. But as Danny told old Mr. Toad, if he were not timid he would not have much of a chance to survive. Besides, he was nimble and quick and his senses were keen. He rather enjoyed playing hide-and-seek with his foe Reddy Fox, darting from one little tunnel to another across the meadow. One day, however, he forgot to look up and Hooty the Owl nearly had a tasty dinner. That adventure brought Peter Rabbit to Danny's aid, and later Danny had the opportunity to return Peter's kindness.

The Adventures of Danny Meadow Mouse, first published in 1915, was the work of author, naturalist and environmentalist Thornton W. Burgess. Born in Sandwich, Massachusetts, in 1874, he wandered the shores, meadows and forests of this Cape Cod town during his boyhood, gaining a love and appreciation of nature that formed the spirit of his later work. From his first book in 1910 to this day, the stories of Thornton W. Burgess have delighted both young and old. But Burgess did more than just entertain: he was careful to present accurately the habits of wild creatures so that readers would also learn from his stories. He further believed that children could gain a better understanding of life by reading about the ways of the animals. It was his aim that those who read his stories would grow to share his love of nature and his concern for the natural environment and its preservation.

Today that aim is the stated goal of the Thornton W. Burgess Society in Sandwich. The Society runs the Thornton W. Burgess Museum, which honors the life and work of this extraordinary man, and the Green Briar Nature Center, which carries out his goals in environmental education and preservation.

Contents

List of Illustrations

I
Danny Meadow Mouse
Is Worried

DANNY MEADOW MOUSE sat on his door-step with his chin in his hands, and it was very plain to see that Danny had something on his mind. He had only a nod for Jimmy Skunk, and even Peter Rabbit could get no more than a grumpy "good morning." It wasn't that he had been caught napping the day before by Reddy Fox and nearly made an end of. No, it wasn't that. Danny had learned his lesson, and Reddy would never catch him again. It wasn't that he was all alone with no one to play with. Danny was rather glad that he was alone. The fact is, Danny Meadow Mouse was worried.

Now worry is one of the worst things in the world, and it didn't seem as if there was anything that Danny Meadow Mouse need worry about. But you know it is the easiest thing in the world to find something to worry over and

1

make yourself uncomfortable about. And when you make yourself uncomfortable, you are almost sure to make every one around you equally uncomfortable. It was so with Danny Meadow Mouse. Striped Chipmunk had twice called him "Cross Patch" that morning, and Johnny Chuck, who had fought Reddy Fox for him the day before, had called him "Grumpy." And what do you think was the matter with Danny Meadow Mouse? Why, he was worrying because his tail is short. Yes, Sir, that is all that ailed Danny Meadow Mouse that bright morning.

You know some people let their looks make them miserable. They worry because they are homely or freckled, or short or tall, or thin or stout, all of which is very foolish. And Danny Meadow Mouse was just as foolish in worrying because his tail is short.

It is short! It certainly is all of that! Danny never had realized how short until he chanced to meet his cousin Whitefoot, who lives in the Green Forest. He was very elegantly dressed, but the most imposing thing about him was his long, slim, beautiful tail. Danny had at once become conscious of his own stubby little tail, and he had hardly had pride enough to hold his head up as became an honest Meadow Mouse. Ever since he had been thinking and thinking, and wondering how his family came to have such short tails. Then he grew envious and began to wish and wish and wish that he could have a long tail like his cousin Whitefoot.

He was so busy wishing that he had a long tail that he quite forgot to take care of the tail he did have, and he pretty nearly lost it and his life with it. Old Whitetail the Marsh Hawk spied Danny sitting there moping on his doorstep, and came sailing over the tops of the meadow grasses so softly that he all but caught Danny. If it hadn't been for one of the Merry Little Breezes, Danny would have been caught. And all because he was envious. It's a bad, bad habit.

II

Danny Meadow Mouse and His Short Tail

ALL DANNY MEADOW MOUSE could think about was his short tail. He was so ashamed of it that whenever any one passed, he crawled out of sight so that they should not see how short his tail is. Instead of playing in the sunshine as he used to do, he sat and sulked. Pretty soon his friends began to pass without stopping. Finally one day old Mr. Toad sat down in front of Danny and began to ask questions.

"What's the matter?" asked old Mr. Toad.

"Nothing," replied Danny Meadow Mouse.

"I don't suppose that there really is anything the matter, but what do you think is the matter?" said old Mr. Toad.

Danny fidgeted, and old Mr. Toad looked up at jolly, round, red Mr. Sun and winked. "Sun is just as bright as ever, isn't it?" he inquired.

"Yes," said Danny.

"Got plenty to eat and drink, haven't you?" continued Mr. Toad.

"Yes," said Danny.

"Seems to me that that is a pretty good looking suit of clothes you're wearing," said Mr. Toad, eyeing Danny critically. "Sunny weather, plenty to eat and drink, and good clothes—must be you don't know when you're well off, Danny Meadow Mouse."

Danny hung his head. Finally he looked up and caught a kindly twinkle in old Mr. Toad's eyes. "Mr. Toad, how can I get a long tail like my cousin Whitefoot of the Green Forest?" he asked.

"Got plenty to eat and drink, haven't you?"
continued Mr. Toad. *Page 4.*

"So that's what's the matter! Ha! ha! ha! Danny Meadow Mouse, I'm ashamed of you! I certainly am ashamed of you!" said Mr. Toad. "What good would a long tail do you? Tell me that."

For a minute Danny didn't know just what to say. "I—I—I'd look so much better if I had a long tail," he ventured.

Old Mr. Toad just laughed. "You never saw a Meadow Mouse with a long tail, did you? Of course not. What a sight it would be! Why, everybody on the Green Meadows would laugh themselves sick at the sight! You see you need to be slim and trim and handsome to carry a long tail well. And then what a nuisance it would be! You would always have to be thinking of your tail and taking care to keep it out of harm's way. Look at me. I'm homely. Some folks call me ugly to look at. But no one tries to catch me as Farmer Brown's boy does Billy Mink because of his fine coat; and no one wants to put me in a cage because of a fine voice. I am satisfied to be just as I am, and if you'll take my advice, Danny Meadow Mouse, you'll be satisfied to be just as you are."

"Perhaps you are right," said Danny Meadow Mouse after a little. "I'll try."

III

Danny Meadow Mouse
Plays Hide and Seek

LIFE IS ALWAYS a game of hide and seek to Danny Meadow Mouse. You see, he is such a fat little fellow that there are a great many other furry-coated people, and almost as many who wear feathers, who would gobble Danny up for breakfast or for dinner if they could. Some of them pretend to be his friends, but Danny always keeps his eyes open when they are around and always begins to play hide and seek. Peter Rabbit and Jimmy Skunk and Striped Chipmunk and Happy Jack Squirrel are all friends whom he can trust, but he always has a bright twinkling eye open for Reddy Fox and Billy Mink and Shadow the Weasel and old Whitetail the Marsh Hawk, and several more, especially Hooty the Owl at night.

Now Danny Meadow Mouse is a stout-hearted little fellow, and when rough Brother North Wind came shouting across the Green Meadows, tearing to pieces the snow clouds and shaking out the snowflakes until they covered the Green Meadows deep, deep, deep, Danny just snuggled down in his warm coat in his snug little house of grass and waited. Danny liked the snow. Yes, Sir, Danny Meadow Mouse liked the snow. He just loved to dig in it and make tunnels. Through those tunnels in every direction he could go where he pleased and when he pleased without being seen by anybody. It was great fun!

Every little way he made a little round doorway up beside a stiff stalk of grass. Out of this he could peep at the white world, and he could get the fresh cold air. Sometimes, when he was quite sure that no one was around, he would scamper across on top of the snow from one doorway to another, and when he did this, he made the prettiest little footprints.

Now Reddy Fox knew all about those doorways and who made them. Reddy was having hard work to get enough to eat this cold weather, and he was hungry most of the time. One morning, as he came tiptoeing softly over the meadows, what should he see just ahead of him but the head of Danny Meadow Mouse pop out of one of those little round doorways. Reddy's mouth watered, and he stole forward more softly than ever. When he got within jumping distance, he drew his stout hind legs

under him and made ready to spring. Presto!
Danny Meadow Mouse had disappeared!
Reddy Fox jumped just the same and began to
dig as fast as he could make his paws go. He
could smell Danny Meadow Mouse and that
made him almost frantic.

All the time Danny Meadow Mouse was
scurrying along one of his little tunnels, and
when finally Reddy Fox stopped digging
because he was quite out of breath, Danny
popped his head out of another little doorway and laughed at Reddy. Of course Reddy
saw him, and of course Reddy tried to catch
him there, and dug frantically just as before.
And of course Danny Meadow Mouse wasn't
there.

After a while Reddy Fox grew tired of this
kind of a game and tried another plan. The
next time he saw Danny Meadow Mouse stick
his head out, Reddy pretended not to see him.
He stretched himself out on the ground and
made believe that he was very tired and
sleepy. He closed his eyes. Then he opened
them just the tiniest bit, so that he could see
Danny Meadow Mouse and yet seem to be
asleep. Danny watched him for a long time.
Then he chuckled to himself and dropped out
of sight.

No sooner was he gone than Reddy Fox

Danny popped his head out of another little
doorway and laughed at Reddy. *Page 9.*

stole over close to the little doorway and waited. "He'll surely stick his head out again to see if I'm asleep, and then I'll have him," said Reddy to himself. So he waited and waited and waited. By and by he turned his head. There was Danny Meadow Mouse at another little doorway laughing at him!

IV

Old Granny Fox Tries for Danny Meadow Mouse

DANNY MEADOW MOUSE had not enjoyed anything so much for a long time as he did that game of hide and seek. He tickled and chuckled all the afternoon as he thought about it. Of course Reddy had been "it." He had been "it" all the time, for never once had he caught Danny Meadow Mouse. If he had—well, there wouldn't have been any more stories about Danny Meadow Mouse, because there wouldn't have been any Danny Meadow Mouse any more.

But Danny never let himself think about this. He had enjoyed the game all the more

because it had been such a dangerous game.
It had been such fun to dive into one of his little round doorways in the snow, run along
one of his own little tunnels, and then peep
out at another doorway and watch Reddy Fox
digging as fast as ever he could at the doorway Danny had just left. Finally Reddy had
given up in disgust and gone off muttering
angrily to try to find something else for dinner. Danny had sat up on the snow and
watched him go. In his funny little squeaky
voice Danny shouted:

> "Though Reddy Fox is smart and sly,
>   Hi-hum-diddle-de-o!
>   I'm just as smart and twice as spry.
>   Hi-hum-diddle-de-o!"

That night Reddy Fox told old Granny Fox
all about how he had tried to catch Danny
Meadow Mouse. Granny listened with her
head cocked on one side. When Reddy told
how fat Danny Meadow Mouse was, her
mouth watered. You see now that snow covered the Green Meadows and the Green Forest, Granny and Reddy Fox had hard work to
get enough to eat, and they were hungry most
of the time.

"I'll go with you down on the meadows to-
morrow morning, and then we'll see if Danny

Meadow Mouse is as smart as he thinks he is," said Granny Fox.

So, bright and early the next morning, old Granny Fox and Reddy Fox went down on the meadows where Danny Meadow Mouse lives. Danny had felt in his bones that Reddy would come back, so he was watching, and he saw them as soon as they came out of the Green Forest. When he saw old Granny Fox, Danny's heart beat a little faster than before, for he knew that Granny Fox is very smart and very wise and has learned most of the tricks of all the other little meadow and forest people.

"This is going to be a more exciting game than the other," said Danny to himself, and scurried down out of sight to see that all his little tunnels were clear so that he could run fast through them if he had to. Then he peeped out of one of his little doorways hidden in a clump of tall grass.

Old Granny Fox set Reddy to hunting for Danny's little round doorways, and as fast as he found them, Granny came up and sniffed at each. She knew that she could tell by the smell which one he had been at last. Finally she came straight towards the tall bunch of grass. Danny ducked down and scurried along one of his little tunnels. He heard Granny Fox sniff at the doorway he had just left. Suddenly something plunged down through the snow right at his very heels. Danny didn't have to look to know that it was Granny Fox herself, and he squeaked with fright.

V

What Happened on the Green Meadows

THICK AND FAST things were happening to Danny Meadow Mouse down on the snow-covered Green Meadows. Rather, they were almost happening. He hadn't minded when Reddy Fox all alone tried to catch him. Indeed, he had made a regular game of hide and seek of it and had enjoyed it immensely. But now it was different. Granny Fox wasn't so easily fooled as Reddy Fox. Just Granny alone would have made the game dangerous for Danny Meadow Mouse. But Reddy was with her, and so Danny had two to look out for, and he got so many frights that it seemed to him as if his heart had moved right up into his mouth and was going to stay there. Yes, Sir, that is just how it seemed.

Down in his little tunnels underneath the snow Danny Meadow Mouse felt perfectly safe from Reddy Fox, who would stop and dig frantically at the little round doorway where he had last seen Danny. But old Granny Fox knew all about those little tunnels, and she didn't waste any time digging at the doorways. Instead she cocked her sharp little ears and listened with all her might. Now Granny Fox has very keen ears, oh, very keen ears, and she heard just what she hoped she would hear. She heard Danny Meadow Mouse running along one of his little tunnels under the snow.

Plunge! Old Granny Fox dived right into the snow and right through into the tunnel of Danny Meadow Mouse. Her two black paws actually touched Danny's tail. He was glad then that it was no longer.

"Ha!" cried Granny Fox, "I almost got him that time!"

Then she ran ahead a little way over the snow, listening as before. Plunge! Into the snow she went again. It was lucky for him that Danny had just turned into another tunnel, for otherwise she would surely have caught him.

Granny Fox blew the snow out of her nose. "Next time I'll get him!" said she.

Now Reddy Fox is quick to learn, especially when it is a way to get something to eat. He watched Granny Fox, and when he understood what she was doing, he made up his mind to have a try himself, for he was afraid that if she caught Danny Meadow Mouse, she would think that he was not big enough to divide. Perhaps that was because Reddy is very selfish himself. So the next time Granny plunged into the snow and missed Danny Meadow Mouse just as before, Reddy rushed in ahead of her, and the minute he heard Danny running down below, he plunged in just as he had seen Granny do. But he didn't take the pains to make sure of just where Danny was, and so of course he didn't come anywhere near him. But he frightened Danny still more and made old Granny Fox lose her temper.

Poor Danny Meadow Mouse! He had never been so frightened in all his life. He didn't know which way to turn or where to run. And so he sat still, which, although he didn't know it, was the very best thing he could do. When he sat still he made no noise, and so of course Granny and Reddy Fox could not tell where he was. Old Granny Fox sat and listened and listened and listened, and wondered where Danny Meadow Mouse was. And down under the snow Danny Meadow Mouse sat and listened and listened and listened, and wondered where Granny and Reddy Fox were.

"Pooh!" said Granny Fox after a while, "that Meadow Mouse thinks he can fool me by sitting still. I'll give him a scare."

Then she began to plunge into the snow this way and that way, and sure enough, pretty soon she landed so close to Danny Meadow Mouse that one of her claws scratched him.

VI

Danny Meadow Mouse Remembers and Reddy Fox Forgets

"THERE HE GOES!" cried old Granny Fox. "Don't let him sit still again!"

"I hear him!" shouted Reddy Fox, and plunged down into the snow just as Granny Fox had done a minute before. But he didn't catch anything, and when he had blown the snow out of his nose and wiped it out of his eyes, he saw Granny Fox dive into the snow with no better luck.

"Never mind," said Granny Fox, "as long as

we keep him running, we can hear him, and some one of these times we'll catch him. Pretty soon he'll get too tired to be so spry, and when he is—" Granny didn't finish, but licked her chops and smacked her lips. Reddy Fox grinned, then licked his chops and smacked his lips. Then once more they took turns diving into the snow.

And down underneath in the little tunnels he had made, Danny Meadow Mouse was running for his life. He was getting tired, just as old Granny Fox had said he would. He was almost out of breath. He was sore and one leg smarted, for in one of her jumps old Granny Fox had so nearly caught him that her claws had torn his pants and scratched him.

"Oh, dear! Oh, dear! If only I had time to think!" panted Danny Meadow Mouse, and then he squealed in still greater fright as Reddy Fox crashed down into his tunnel right at his very heels. "I've got to get somewhere! I've got to get somewhere where they can't get at me!" he sobbed. And right that very instant he remembered the old fence-post!

The old fence-post lay on the ground and was hollow. Fastened to it were long wires with sharp cruel barbs. Danny had made a tunnel over to that old fence-post the very first day after the snow came, for in that hollow in the old post he had a secret store of seeds. Why hadn't he thought of it before? It must have been because he was too frightened to think. But he remembered now, and he dodged into the tunnel that led to the old fence-post, running faster than ever, for though his heart was in his mouth from fear, in his heart was hope, and hope is a wonderful thing.

Now old Granny Fox knew all about that old fence-post and she remembered all about those barbed wires fastened to it. Although they were covered with snow she knew just about where they lay, and just before she reached them she stopped plunging down into the snow. Reddy Fox knew about those wires, too, but he was so excited that he forgot all about them.

"Stop!" cried old Granny Fox sharply.

But Reddy Fox didn't hear, or if he heard he didn't heed. His sharp ears could hear Danny Meadow Mouse running almost underneath him. Granny Fox could stop if she wanted to, but he was going to have Danny Meadow Mouse for his breakfast! Down into the snow he plunged as hard as ever he could.

"Oh! Oh! Wow! Wow! Oh, dear! Oh, dear!"

That wasn't the voice of Danny Meadow Mouse. Oh, my, no! It was the voice of Reddy

Fox. Yes, Sir, it was the voice of Reddy Fox. He had landed with one of his black paws right on one of those sharp wire barbs, and it did hurt dreadfully.

"I never did know a young Fox who could get into so much trouble as you can!" snapped old Granny Fox, as Reddy hobbled along on three legs behind her, across the snow-covered Green Meadows. "It serves you right for forgetting!"

"Yes'm," said Reddy meekly.

And safe in the hollow of the old fence-post, Danny Meadow Mouse was dressing the scratch on his leg made by the claws of old Granny Fox.

VII

Old Granny Fox Tries a New Plan

OLD GRANNY FOX kept thinking about Danny Meadow Mouse. She knew that he was fat, and it made her mouth water every time she thought of him. She made up her mind that she must and would have him. She

knew that Danny had been very, very much
frightened when she and Reddy Fox had tried
so hard to catch him by plunging down
through the snow into his little tunnels after
him, and she felt pretty sure that he wouldn't
go far away from the old fence-post, in the
hollow of which he was snug and safe.

Old Granny Fox is very smart. "Danny
Meadow Mouse won't put his nose out of that
old fence-post for a day or two. Then he'll get
tired of staying inside all the time, and he'll
peep out of one of his little round doorways
to see if the way is clear. If he doesn't see any
danger, he'll come out and run around on top
of the snow to get some of the seeds in the
tops of the tall grasses that stick out through
the snow. If nothing frightens him, he'll keep
going a little farther and a little farther from
that old fence-post. I must see to it that Danny
Meadow Mouse isn't frightened for a few
days." So said old Granny Fox to herself, as
she lay under a hemlock-tree, studying how
she could best get the next meal.

Then she called Reddy Fox to her and for-
bade him to go down on the meadows until
she should tell him he might. Reddy grumbled
and mumbled and didn't see why he shouldn't
go where he pleased, but he didn't dare disobey. You see he had a sore foot. He had hurt

it on a wire barb when he was plunging through the snow after Danny Meadow Mouse, and now he had to run on three legs. That meant that he must depend upon Granny Fox to help him get enough to eat. So Reddy didn't dare to disobey.

It all came out just as Granny Fox had thought it would. Danny Meadow Mouse *did* get tired of staying in the old fence-post. He *did* peep out first, and then he *did* run a little way on the snow, and then a little farther and a little farther. But all the time he took great care not to get more than a jump or two from one of his little round doorways leading down to his tunnels under the snow.

Hidden on the edge of the Green Forest, Granny Fox watched him. She looked up at the sky, and she knew that it was going to snow again. "That's good," said she. "To-morrow morning I'll have fat Meadow Mouse for breakfast," and she smiled a hungry smile.

The next morning, before jolly, round, red Mr. Sun was out of bed, old Granny Fox trotted down on to the meadows and straight over to where, down under the snow, lay the old fence-post. It had snowed again, and all of the little doorways of Danny Meadow Mouse were covered up with soft, fleecy snow. Behind Granny Fox limped Reddy Fox, grumbling to himself.

When they reached the place where the old fence-post lay buried under the snow, old Granny Fox stretched out as flat as she could. Then she told Reddy to cover her up with the new soft snow. Reddy did as he was told, but all the time he grumbled. "Now you go off to the Green Forest and keep out of sight," said Granny Fox. "By and by I'll bring you some Meadow Mouse for your breakfast," and Granny Fox chuckled to think how smart she was and how she was going to catch Danny Meadow Mouse.

VIII

Brother North Wind Proves a Friend

DANNY MEADOW MOUSE had seen nothing of old Granny Fox or Reddy Fox for several days. Every morning the first thing he did, even before he had breakfast, was to climb up to one of his little round doorways and peep out over the beautiful white meadows, to see if there was any danger near. But every time he did this, Danny used a different doorway. "For," said Danny to himself, "if any one should happen, just happen, to see me this morning, they might be waiting just outside my doorway to catch me to-morrow morning." You see there is a great deal of wisdom in the little head that Danny Meadow Mouse carries on his shoulders.

But the first day and the second day and the third day he saw nothing of old Granny Fox or of Reddy Fox, and he began to enjoy running through his tunnels under the snow and scurrying across from one doorway to another on top of the snow, just as he had before the Foxes had tried so hard to catch him. But he hadn't forgotten, as Granny Fox had hoped he would. No, indeed, Danny Meadow Mouse hadn't forgotten. He was too wise for that.

One morning, when he started to climb up to one of his little doorways, he found that it was closed. Yes, Sir, it was closed. In fact, there wasn't any doorway. More snow had fallen from the clouds in the night and had covered up every one of the little round doorways of Danny Meadow Mouse.

"Ha!" said Danny, "I shall have a busy day, a very busy day, opening all my doorways. I'll eat my breakfast, and then I'll go to work."

So Danny Meadow Mouse ate a good breakfast of seeds which he had stored in the hollow in the old fence-post buried under the

snow, and then he began work on the nearest
doorway. It really wasn't work at all, for you
see the snow was soft and light, and Danny
dearly loved to dig in it. In a few minutes he
had made a wee hole through which he could
peep up at jolly, round Mr. Sun. In a few minutes more he had made it big enough to put
his head out. He looked this way and he
looked that way. Far, far off on the top of a
tree he could see old Roughleg the Hawk, but
he was so far away that Danny didn't fear him
at all.

"I don't see anything or anybody to be
afraid of," said Danny and poked his head out
a little farther.

Then he sat and studied everything around
him a long, long time. It was a beautiful white
world, a very beautiful white world. Everything was so white and pure and beautiful
that it didn't seem possible that harm or danger for any one could even be thought of. But
Danny Meadow Mouse learned long ago that
things are not always what they seem, and so
he sat with just his little head sticking out of
his doorway and studied and studied. Just a
little way off was a little heap of snow.

"I don't remember that," said Danny. "And I
don't remember anything that would make
that. There isn't any little bush or old log or

anything underneath it. Perhaps rough Brother North Wind heaped it up, just for fun."

But all the time Danny Meadow Mouse kept studying and studying that little heap of snow. Pretty soon he saw rough Brother North Wind coming his way and tossing the snow about as he came. He caught a handful from the top of the little heap of snow that Danny was studying, and when he had passed, Danny's sharp eyes saw something red there. It was just the color of the cloak old Granny Fox wears.

> "Granny Fox, you can't fool me!
> I see you plain as plain can be!"

shouted Danny Meadow Mouse and dropped down out of sight, while old Granny Fox shook the snow from her red cloak and, with a snarl of disappointment and anger, slowly started for the Green Forest, where Reddy Fox was waiting for her.

IX

Danny Meadow Mouse
Is Caught at Last

"Tippy-toppy-tippy-toe,
  Play and frolic in the snow!
  Now you see me! Now you don't!
  Think you'll catch me, but you won't!
  Tippy-toppy-tippy-toe,
  Oh, such fun to play in snow!"

DANNY MEADOW MOUSE sang this, or at
least he tried to sing it, as he skipped
about on the snow that covered the Green
Meadows. But Danny Meadow Mouse has
such a little voice, such a funny little squeaky
voice, that had you been there you probably
would never have guessed that he was singing. He thought he was, though, and was
enjoying it just as much as if he had the most
beautiful voice in the world. You know singing
is nothing in the world but happiness in the
heart making itself heard.

Oh, yes, Danny Meadow Mouse was happy!
Why shouldn't he have been? Hadn't he
proved himself smarter than old Granny Fox?
That is something to make any one happy.

Some folks may fool Granny Fox once; some may fool her twice; but there are very few who can keep right on fooling her until she gives up in disgust. That is just what Danny Meadow Mouse had done, and he felt very smart and of course he felt very happy.

So Danny sang his little song and skipped about in the moonlight, and dodged in and out of his little round doorways, and all the time kept his sharp little eyes open for any sign of Granny Fox or Reddy Fox. But with all his smartness, Danny forgot. Yes, Sir, Danny forgot one thing. He forgot to watch up in the sky. He knew that of course old Roughleg the Hawk was asleep, so he had nothing to fear from him. But he never once thought of Hooty the Owl.

Dear me, dear me! Forgetting is a dreadful habit. If nobody ever forgot, there wouldn't be nearly so much trouble in the world. No, indeed, there wouldn't be nearly so much trouble. And Danny Meadow Mouse forgot. He skipped and sang and was happy as could be, and never once thought to watch up in the sky.

Over in the Green Forest Hooty the Owl had had poor hunting, and he was feeling cross. You see, Hooty was hungry, and hunger is apt to make one feel cross. The longer he hunted, the hungrier and crosser he grew. Suddenly he thought of Danny Meadow Mouse.

"I suppose he is asleep somewhere safe and snug under the snow," grumbled Hooty, "but he might be, he just *might* be out for a frolic in the moonlight. I believe I'll go down on the meadows and see."

Now Hooty the Owl can fly without making the teeniest, weeniest sound. It seems as if he just drifts along through the air like a great shadow. Now he spread his great wings and floated out over the meadows. You know Hooty can see as well at night as most folks can by day, and it was not long before he saw Danny Meadow Mouse skipping about on the snow and dodging in and out of his little round doorways. Hooty's great eyes grew brighter and fiercer. Without a sound he floated through the moonlight until he was just over Danny Meadow Mouse.

Too late Danny looked up. His little song ended in a tiny squeak of fear, and he started for his nearest little round doorway. Hooty the Owl reached down with his long cruel claws and—Danny Meadow Mouse was caught at last!

X

A Strange Ride and
How It Ended

DANNY MEADOW MOUSE often had sat watching Skimmer the Swallow sailing around up in the blue, blue sky. He had watched Ol' Mistah Buzzard go up, up, up, until he was nothing but a tiny speck, and Danny had wondered how it would seem to be way up above the Green Meadows and the Green Forest and look down. It had seemed to him that it must be very wonderful and beautiful. Sometimes he had wished that he had wings and could go up in the air and look down. And now here he was, he, Danny Meadow Mouse, actually doing that very thing!

But Danny could see nothing wonderful or beautiful now. No, indeed! Everything was terrible, for you see Danny Meadow Mouse wasn't flying himself. He was being carried. Yes, Sir, Danny Meadow Mouse was being carried through the air in the cruel claws of Hooty the Owl! And all because Danny had forgotten—forgotten to watch up in the sky for danger.

He was being carried. *Page 30.*

Poor, poor Danny Meadow Mouse! Hooty's great cruel claws hurt him dreadfully! But it wasn't the pain that was the worst. No, indeed! It wasn't the pain! It was the thought of what would happen when Hooty reached his home in the Green Forest, for he knew that there Hooty would gobble him up, bones and all. As he flew, Hooty kept chuckling, and Danny Meadow Mouse knew just what those chuckles meant. They meant that Hooty was thinking of the good meal he was going to have.

Hanging there in Hooty's great cruel claws, Danny looked down on the snow-covered Green Meadows he loved so well. They seemed a frightfully long way below him, though really they were not far at all, for Hooty was flying very low. But Danny Meadow Mouse had never in all his life been so high up before, and so it seemed to him that he was way, way up in the sky, and he shut his eyes so as not to see. But he couldn't keep them shut. No, Sir, he couldn't keep them shut! He just *had* to keep opening them. There was the dear old Green Forest drawing nearer and nearer. It always had looked very beautiful to Danny Meadow Mouse, but now it looked terrible, very terrible indeed, because over in it, in some dark place, was the home of Hooty the Owl.

Just ahead of him was the Old Briar-patch where Peter Rabbit lives so safely. Every old bramble in it was covered with snow and it was very, very beautiful. Really everything was just as beautiful as ever—the moonlight, the Green Forest, the snow-covered Green Meadows, the Old Briar-patch. The only change was in Danny Meadow Mouse himself, and it was all because he had forgotten.

Suddenly Danny began to wriggle and struggle. "Keep still!" snapped Hooty the Owl.

But Danny only struggled harder than ever. It seemed to him that Hooty wasn't holding him as tightly as at first. He felt one of Hooty's claws slip. It tore his coat and hurt dreadfully, but it slipped! The fact is, Hooty had only grabbed Danny Meadow Mouse by the loose part of his coat, and up in the air he couldn't get hold of Danny any better. Danny kicked, squirmed and twisted, and twisted, squirmed, and kicked. He felt his coat tear and of course the skin with it, but he kept right on, for now he was hanging almost free. Hooty had started down now, so as to get a better hold. Danny gave one more kick and then—he felt himself falling!

Danny Meadow Mouse shut his eyes and held his breath. Down, down, down he fell. It seemed to him that he never would strike the snow-covered meadows! Really he fell only a

very little distance. But it seemed a terrible
distance to Danny. He hit something that
scratched him, and then plump! he landed in
the soft snow right in the very middle of the
Old Briar-patch, and the last thing he remembered was hearing the scream of disappointment and rage of Hooty the Owl.

XI

Peter Rabbit Gets a Fright

PETER RABBIT sat in his favorite place in
the middle of the dear Old Briar-patch,
trying to decide which way he would go on
his travels that night. The night before he had
had a narrow escape from old Granny Fox
over in the Green Forest. There was nothing
to eat around the Smiling Pool and no one to
talk to there any more, and you know that
Peter must either eat or ask questions in
order to be perfectly happy. No, the Smiling
Pool was too dull a place to interest Peter on
such a beautiful moonlight night, and Peter
had no mind to try his legs against those of
Old Granny Fox again in the Green Forest.

Early that morning, just after Peter had settled down for his morning nap, Tommy Tit the Chickadee had dropped into the dear Old Briar-patch just to be neighborly. Peter was just dozing off when he heard the cheeriest little voice in the world. It was saying:

"Dee-dee-chickadee!
I see you! Can you see me?"

Peter began to smile even before he could get his eyes open and look up. There, right over his head, was Tommy Tit hanging head down from a nodding old bramble. In a twinkling he was down on the snow right in front of Peter, then up in the brambles again, right side up, upside down, here, there, everywhere, never still a minute, and all the time chattering away in the cheeriest little voice in the world.

"Dee-dee-chickadee!
I'm as happy as can be!
Find it much the better way
To be happy all the day.
Dee-dee-chickadee!
Everybody's good to me!"

"Hello, Tommy!" said Peter Rabbit. "Where'd you come from?"

"From Farmer Brown's new orchard up on the hill. It's a fine orchard, Peter Rabbit, a fine orchard. I go there every morning for my breakfast. If the winter lasts long enough, I'll have all the trees cleaned up for Farmer Brown."

Peter looked puzzled. "What do you mean?" he asked.

"Just what I say," replied Tommy Tit, almost turning a somersault in the air. "There's a million eggs of insects on those young peach-trees, but I'm clearing them all off as fast as I can. They're mighty fine eating, Peter Rabbit, mighty fine eating!" And with that Tommy Tit had said good-by and flitted away.

Peter was thinking of that young orchard now, as he sat in the moonlight trying to make up his mind where to go. The thought of those young peach-trees made his mouth water. It was a long way up to the orchard on the hill, a very long way, and Peter was wondering if it really was safe to go. He had just about made up his mind to try it, for Peter is very, very fond of the bark of young peach-trees, when thump! something dropped out of the sky at his very feet.

It startled Peter so that he nearly tumbled over backward. And right at the same instant came the fierce, angry scream of Hooty the

Owl. That almost made Peter's heart stop beating, although he knew that Hooty couldn't get him down there in the Old Briar-patch. When Peter got his wits together and his heart didn't go so jumpy, he looked to see what had dropped so close to him out of the sky. His big eyes grew bigger than ever, and he rubbed them to make quite sure that he really saw what he thought he saw. Yes, there was no doubt about it—there at his feet lay Danny Meadow Mouse!

XII

The Old Briar-patch Has a New Tenant

DANNY MEADOW MOUSE slowly opened his eyes and then closed them again quickly, as if afraid to look around. He could hear some one talking. It was a pleasant voice, not at all like the terrible voice of Hooty the Owl, which was the very last thing that Danny Meadow Mouse could remember. Danny lay still a minute and listened.

"Why, Danny Meadow Mouse, where in the

world did you drop from?" asked the voice. It sounded like—why, very much like Peter Rabbit speaking. Danny opened his eyes again. It *was* Peter Rabbit.

"Where—where am I?" asked Danny Meadow Mouse in a very weak and small voice.

"In the middle of the dear Old Briar-patch with me," replied Peter Rabbit. "But how did you get here? You seemed to drop right out of the sky."

Danny Meadow Mouse shuddered. Suddenly he remembered everything: how Hooty the Owl had caught him in great cruel claws and had carried him through the moonlight across the snow-covered Green Meadows; how he had felt Hooty's claws slip and then had struggled and kicked and twisted and turned until his coat had torn and he had dropped down, down, down until he had landed in the soft snow and knocked all the breath out of his little body. The very last thing he could remember was Hooty's fierce scream of rage and disappointment. Danny shuddered again.

Then a new thought came to him. He must get out of sight! Hooty might catch him again! Danny tried to scramble to his feet.

"Ooch! Oh!" groaned Danny and lay still again.

"There, there. Keep still, Danny Meadow Mouse. There's nothing to be afraid of here," said Peter Rabbit gently. His big eyes filled with tears as he looked at Danny Meadow Mouse, for Danny was all torn and hurt by the cruel claws of Hooty the Owl, and you know Peter has a very tender heart.

So Danny lay still, and while Peter Rabbit tried to make him comfortable and dress his hurts, he told Peter all about how he had forgotten to watch up in the sky and so had been caught by Hooty the Owl, and all about his terrible ride in Hooty's cruel claws.

"Oh, dear, whatever shall I do now?" he ended. "However shall I get back home to my warm house of grass, my safe little tunnels under the snow, and my little store of seeds in the snug hollow in the old fence-post?"

Peter Rabbit looked thoughtful. "You can't do it," said he. "You simply can't do it. It is such a long way for a little fellow like you that it wouldn't be safe to try. If you went at night, Hooty the Owl might catch you again. If you tried in daylight, old Roughleg the Hawk would be almost sure to see you. And night or day old Granny Fox or Reddy Fox might come snooping around, and if they did, they would be sure to catch you. I tell you what, you stay right here! The dear Old Briar-patch is the safest place in the world. Why, just think, here you can come out in broad daylight and laugh at Granny and Reddy Fox and at old Roughleg the Hawk, because the good old brambles will keep them out, if they try to get you. You can make just as good tunnels under the snow here as you had there, and there are lots and lots of seeds on the ground to eat. You know I don't care for them myself. I'm lonesome sometimes, living here all alone. You stay here, and we'll have the Old Briar-patch to ourselves."

Danny Meadow Mouse looked at Peter gratefully. "I will, and thank you ever so much, Peter Rabbit," he said.

And this is how the dear Old Briar-patch happened to have another tenant.

XIII

Peter Rabbit Visits
the Peach Orchard

"DON'T GO, Peter Rabbit! Don't go!" begged Danny Meadow Mouse.

Peter hopped to the edge of the Old Briar-patch and looked over the moonlit, snow-covered meadows to the hill back of Farmer Brown's house. On that hill was the young peach orchard of which Tommy Tit the Chickadee had told him, and ever since Peter's mouth had watered and watered every time he thought of those young peach-trees and the tender bark on them.

"I think I will, Danny, just this once," said Peter. "It's a long way, and I've never been there before; but I guess it's just as safe as the Meadows or the Green Forest.

> "Oh I'm as bold as bold can be!
> Sing hoppy-hippy-hippy-hop-o!
> I'll hie me forth the world to see!
> Sing hoppy-hippy-hippy-hop-o!
> My ears are long,
> My legs are strong,
> So now good day;
> I'll hie away!
> Sing hoppy-hippy-hippy-hop-o!"

And with that, Peter Rabbit left the dear safe Old Briar-patch, and away he went lipperty-lipperty-lip, across the Green Meadows towards the hill and the young orchard back of Farmer Brown's house.

Danny Meadow Mouse watched him go and shook his head in disapproval. "Foolish, foolish, foolish!" he said over and over to himself.

"Why can't Peter be content with the good things that he has?"

Peter Rabbit hurried along through the moonlight, stopping every few minutes to sit up to look and listen. He heard the fierce hunting call of Hooty the Owl way over in the Green Forest, so he felt sure that at present there was nothing to fear from him. He knew that since their return to the Green Meadows and the Green Forest, Granny and Reddy Fox had kept away from Farmer Brown's, so he did not worry about them.

All in good time Peter came to the young orchard. It was just as Tommy Tit the Chickadee had told him. Peter hopped up to the nearest peach-tree and nibbled the bark. My, how good it tasted! He went all around the tree, stripping off the bark. He stood up on his long hind legs and reached as high as he could. Then he dug the snow away and ate down as far as he could. When he could get no more tender young bark, he went on to the next tree.

Now though Peter didn't know it, he was in the very worst kind of mischief. You see, when he took off all the bark all the way around the young peach-tree he killed the tree, for you know it is on the inside of the bark that the sap which gives life to a tree and

makes it grow goes up from the roots to all
the branches. So when Peter ate the bark all
the way around the trunk of the young tree,
he had made it impossible for the sap to come
up in the spring. Oh, it was the very worst
kind of mischief that Peter Rabbit was in.

But Peter didn't know it, and he kept right
on filling that big stomach of his and enjoying
it so much that he forgot to watch out for danger. Suddenly, just as he had begun on another
tree, a great roar right behind him made him
jump almost out of his skin. He knew that
voice, and without waiting to even look
behind him, he started for the stone wall on
the other side of the orchard. Right at his
heels, his great mouth wide open, was Bowser
the Hound.

XIV

Farmer Brown Sets a Trap

PETER RABBIT was in trouble. He had got-
ten into mischief and now, like every one
who gets into mischief, he wished that he
hadn't. The worst of it was that he was a long

way from his home in the dear Old Briar-patch, and he didn't know how he ever could get back there again. Where was he? Why, in the stone wall on one side of Farmer Brown's young peach orchard. How Peter blessed the old stone wall in which he had found a safe hiding-place! Bowser had hung around nearly all night, so that Peter had not dared to try to go home. Now it was daylight, and Peter knew it would not be safe to put his nose outside.

Peter was worried, so worried that he couldn't go to sleep as he usually does in the daytime. So he sat hidden in the old wall and waited and watched. By and by he saw Farmer Brown and Farmer Brown's boy come out into the orchard. Right away they saw the mischief which Peter had done, and he could tell by the sound of their voices that they were very, very angry. They went away, but before long they were back again, and all day long Peter watched them work putting some-thing around each of the young peach-trees. Peter grew so curious that he forgot all about his troubles and how far away from home he was. He could hardly wait for night to come so that he might see what they had been doing.

Just as jolly, round, red Mr. Sun started to

go to bed behind the Purple Hills, Farmer Brown and his boy started back to the house. Farmer Brown was smiling now.

"I guess that that will fix him!" he said.

"Now what does he mean by that?" thought Peter. "Who will it fix? Can it be me? I don't need any fixing."

He waited just as long as he could. When all was still, and the moonlight had begun to make shadows of the trees on the snow, Peter very cautiously crept out of his hiding-place. Bowser the Hound was nowhere in sight, and everything was as quiet and peaceful as it had been when he first came into the orchard the night before. Peter had fully made up his mind to go straight home as fast as his long legs would take him, but his dreadful curiosity insisted that first he must find out what Farmer Brown and his boy had been doing to the young peach-trees.

So Peter hurried over to the nearest tree. All around the trunk of the tree, from the ground clear up higher than Peter could reach, was wrapped wire netting. Peter couldn't get so much as a nibble of the delicious bark. He hadn't intended to take any, for he had meant to go right straight home, but now that he couldn't get any, he wanted some more than ever,—just a bite. Peter looked around. Everything was quiet. He would try the next tree, and then he would go home.

But the next tree was wrapped with wire. Peter hesitated, looked around, turned to go home, thought of how good that bark had tasted the night before, hesitated again, and then hurried over to the third tree. It was protected just like the others. Then Peter forgot all about going home. He wanted some of that delicious bark, and he ran from one tree to another as fast as he could go.

At last, way down at the end of the orchard, Peter found a tree that had no wire around it. "They must have forgotten this one!" he thought, and his eyes sparkled. All around on the snow were a lot of little, shiny wires, but Peter didn't notice them. All he saw was that delicious bark on the young peach-tree. He hopped right into the middle of the wires, and then, just as he reached up to take the first bite of bark, he felt something tugging at one of his hind legs.

XV

Peter Rabbit Is
Caught in a Snare

WHEN PETER RABBIT, reaching up to nibble the bark of one of Farmer Brown's young trees, felt something tugging at one of his hind legs, he was so startled that he jumped to get away. Instead of doing this, he fell flat on his face. The thing on his hind leg had tightened and held him fast. A great fear came to Peter Rabbit, and lying there in the snow, he kicked and struggled with all his might. But the more he kicked, the tighter grew that hateful thing on his leg! Finally he grew too tired to kick any more and lay still. The dreadful thing that held him hurt his leg, but it didn't pull when he lay still.

When he had grown a little calmer, Peter sat up to examine the thing which held him so fast. It was something like one of the blackberry vines he had sometimes tripped over, only it was bright and shiny, and had no branches or tiny prickers, and one end was fastened to a stake. Peter tried to bite off the shiny thing, but even his great, sharp front teeth couldn't cut it. Then Peter knew what it was. It was wire! It was a snare which Farmer Brown had set to catch him, and which he had walked right into because he had been so greedy for the bark of the young peach-tree that he had not used his eyes to look out for danger.

Oh, how Peter Rabbit did wish that he had not been so curious to know what Farmer Brown had been doing that day, and that he had gone straight home as he had meant to do, instead of trying to get one more meal of young peach-bark! Big tears rolled down Peter's cheeks. What should he do? What *could* he do? For a long time Peter sat in the moonlight, trying to think of something to do. At last he thought of the stake to which that hateful wire was fastened. The stake was of wood, and Peter's teeth would cut wood. Peter's heart gave a great leap of hope, and he began at once to dig away the snow from around the stake, and then settled himself to gnaw the stake in two.

Peter had been hard at work on the stake a long time and had it a little more than half cut through, when he heard a loud sniff down at the other end of the orchard. He looked up to see—whom do you think? Why, Bowser the Hound! He hadn't seen Peter yet, but he had already found Peter's tracks, and it wouldn't be but a few minutes before he found Peter himself.

Poor Peter Rabbit! There wasn't time to finish cutting off the stake. What could he do? He made a frightened jump just as he had when he first felt the wire tugging at his leg. Just as before, he was thrown flat on his face. He scrambled to his feet and jumped again, only to be thrown just as before. Just then Bowser the Hound saw him and opening his mouth sent forth a great roar. Peter made one more frantic jump. Snap! the stake had broken! Peter pitched forward on his head, turned a somersault, and scrambled to his feet. He was free at last! That is, he could run, but after him dragged a piece of the stake.

How Peter did run! It was hard work, for you know he had to drag that piece of stake after him. But he did it, and just in time he crawled into the old stone wall on one side of the orchard, while Bowser the Hound barked his disappointment to the moon.

XVI

Peter Rabbit's Hard Journey

PETER RABBIT sat in the old stone wall along one side of Farmer Brown's orchard, waiting for Mrs. Moon to put out her light and leave the world in darkness until jolly, round, red Mr. Sun should kick off his rosy bedclothes and begin his daily climb up in the blue, blue sky. In the winter, Mr. Sun is a late sleeper, and Peter knew that there would be two or three hours after Mrs. Moon put out her light when it would be quite dark. And Peter also knew too that by this time Hooty the Owl would probably have caught his dinner. So would old Granny Fox and Reddy Fox. Bowser the Hound would be too sleepy to be on the watch. It would be the very safest time for Peter to try to get to his home in the dear Old Briar-patch.

So Peter waited and waited. Twice Bowser the Hound, who had chased him into the old wall, came over and barked at him and tried to get at him. But the old wall kept Peter safe, and Bowser gave it up. And all the time Peter sat waiting he was in great pain. You see that shiny wire was drawn so tight that it cut into his flesh and hurt dreadfully, and to the other end of the wire was fastened a piece of wood, part of the stake to which the snare had been made fast and which Peter had managed to gnaw and break off.

It was on account of this that Peter was waiting for Mrs. Moon to put out her light. He knew that with that stake dragging after him he would have to go very slowly, and he could not run any more risk of danger than he actually had to. So he waited and waited, and by and by, sure enough, Mrs. Moon put out her light. Peter waited a little longer, listening with all his might. Everything was still. Then Peter crept out of the old stone wall.

Right away trouble began. The stake dragging at the end of the wire fast to his leg caught among the stones and pulled Peter up short. My, how it did hurt! It made the tears come. But Peter shut his teeth hard, and turning back, he worked until he got the stake free. Then he started on once more, dragging the stake after him.

Very slowly across the orchard and under the fence on the other side crept Peter Rabbit, his leg so stiff and sore that he could hardly touch it to the snow, and all the time dragging that piece of stake, which seemed to grow heavier and harder to drag every minute. Peter did not dare to go out across the open fields, for fear some danger might happen along, and he would have no place to hide. So he crept along close to the fences where bushes grow, and this made it very, very hard, for the dragging stake was forever catching in the bushes with a yank at the sore leg which brought Peter up short with a squeal of pain.

This was bad enough, but all the time Peter was filled with a dreadful fear that Hooty the Owl or Granny Fox might just happen along. He had to stop to rest very, very often, and then he would listen and listen. Over and over again he said to himself:

"Oh, dear, whatever did I go up to the young peach orchard for when I knew I had no business there? Why couldn't I have been content with all the good things that were mine in the Green Forest and on the Green Meadows? Oh, dear! Oh, dear!"

Just as jolly, round, red Mr. Sun began to light up the Green Meadows, Peter Rabbit reached the dear Old Briar-patch. Danny Meadow Mouse was sitting on the edge of it anxiously watching for him. Peter crawled up and started to creep in along one of his little private paths. He got in himself, but the dragging stake caught among the brambles, and

Peter just fell down in the snow right where he was, too tired and worn out to move.

XVII

Danny Meadow Mouse Becomes Worried

DANNY MEADOW MOUSE limped around through the dear Old Briar-patch, where he had lived with Peter Rabbit ever since he had squirmed out of the claws of Hooty the Owl and dropped there, right at the feet of Peter Rabbit. Danny limped because he was still lame and sore from Hooty's terrible claws, but he didn't let himself think much about that, because he was so thankful to be alive at all. So he limped around in the Old Briar-patch, picking up seed which had fallen on the snow, and sometimes pulling down a few of the red berries which cling all winter to the wild rose bushes. The seeds in these were very nice indeed, and Danny always felt especially good after a meal of them.

Danny Meadow Mouse had grown very fond of Peter Rabbit, for Peter had been very, very good to him. Danny felt that he never, never could repay all of Peter's kindness. It had been very good of Peter to offer to share the Old Briar-patch with Danny, because Danny was so far from his own home that it would not be safe for him to try to get back there. But Peter had done more than that. He had taken care of Danny, such good care, during the first few days after Danny's escape from Hooty the Owl. He had brought good things to eat while Danny was too weak and sore to get things for himself. Oh, Peter had been very good indeed to him!

But now, as Danny limped around, he was not happy. No, Sir, he was not happy. The truth is, Danny Meadow Mouse was worried. It was a different kind of worry from any he had known before. You see, for the first time in his life, Danny was worrying about some one else. He was worrying about Peter Rabbit. Peter had been gone from the Old Briar-patch a whole night and a whole day. He often was gone all night, but never all day too. Danny was sure that something had happened to Peter. He thought of how he had begged Peter not to go up to Farmer Brown's young peach orchard. He had felt in his bones that it was not safe, that something dreadful would happen to Peter. How Peter had laughed at him and bravely started off! Why hadn't he come home?

As he limped around, Danny talked to himself:

"Why cannot people be content
   With all the good things that are sent,
   And mind their own affairs at home
   Instead of going forth to roam?"

It was now the second night since Peter Rabbit had gone away. Danny Meadow Mouse couldn't sleep at all. Round and round through the Old Briar-patch he limped, and finally sat down at the edge of it to wait and watch. At last, just as jolly, round, red Mr. Sun sent his first long rays of light across the Green Meadows, Danny saw something crawling towards the Old Briar-patch. He rubbed his eyes and looked again. It was—no, it couldn't be—yes, it *was* Peter Rabbit! But what was the matter with him? Always before Peter had come home lipperty-lipperty-lipperty-lip, but now he was crawling, actually *crawling!* Danny Meadow Mouse didn't know what to make of it.

Nearer and nearer came Peter. Something was following him. No, Peter was dragging something after him. At last Peter started to crawl along one of his little private paths into

the Old Briar-patch. The thing dragging behind caught in the brambles, and Peter fell
headlong in the snow, too tired and worn out
to move. Then Danny saw what the trouble
was. A wire was fast to one of Peter's long
hind legs, and to the other end of the wire was
fastened part of a stake. Peter had been
caught in a snare! Danny hurried over to Peter
and tears stood in his eyes.

"Poor Peter Rabbit! Oh, I'm so sorry, Peter!"
he whispered.

XVIII

Danny Meadow Mouse
Returns a Kindness

THERE PETER RABBIT LAY. He had
dragged that piece of stake a long way, a
very long way, indeed. But now he could drag
it no farther, for it had caught in the bramble
bushes. So Peter just dropped on the snow
and cried. Yes, Sir, he cried! You see he was so
tired and worn out and frightened, and his leg
was so stiff and sore and hurt him so! And
then it was so dreadful to actually get home

and be stopped right on your very own door-step. So Peter just lay there and cried. Just supposing old Granny Fox should come poking around and find Peter caught that way! All she would have to do would be to get hold of that hateful stake caught in the bramble bushes and pull Peter out where she could get him. Do you wonder that Peter cried?

By and by he became aware that some one was wiping away his tears. It was Danny Meadow Mouse. And Danny was singing in a funny little voice. Pretty soon Peter stopped crying and listened, and this is what he heard:

> "Isn't any use to cry!
>   Not a bit! Not a bit!
> Wipe your eyes and wipe 'em dry!
>   Use your wit! Use your wit!
> Just remember that to-morrow
> Never brings a single sorrow.
> Yesterday has gone forever
> And to-morrow gets here never.
> Chase your worries all away;
> Nothing's worse than just to-day."

Peter smiled in spite of himself.

"That's right! That's right! Smile away, Peter Rabbit. Smile away! Your troubles, Sir, are all to-day. And between you and me, I don't believe they are so bad as you think they are.

Now you lie still just where you are, while I go see what can be done."

With that off whisked Danny Meadow Mouse as spry as you please, in spite of his lame leg, and in a few minutes Peter knew by little twitches of the wire on his leg that Danny was doing something at the other end. He was. Danny Meadow Mouse had set out to gnaw that piece of stake all to splinters. So there he sat and gnawed and gnawed and gnawed. Jolly, round, red Mr. Sun climbed higher and higher in the sky, and Danny Meadow Mouse grew hungry, but still he kept right on gnawing at that bothersome stake.

By and by, happening to look across the snow-covered Green Meadows, he saw something that made his heart jump. It was Farmer Brown's boy coming straight over towards the dear Old Briar-patch. Danny didn't say a word to Peter Rabbit, but gnawed faster than ever.

Farmer Brown's boy was almost there when Danny stopped gnawing. There was only a tiny bit of the stake left now, and Danny hurried to tell Peter Rabbit that there was nothing to stop him now from going to his most secret retreat in the very heart of the Old Briar-patch. While Peter slowly dragged his way along, Danny trotted behind to see that the wire did not catch on the bushes. They

Peter knew that Danny was doing something
at the other end. *Page 58*.

had safely reached Peter Rabbit's secretest retreat when Farmer Brown's boy came up to the edge of the dear Old Briar-patch.

"So this is where that rabbit that killed our peach-tree lives!" said he. "We'll try a few snares and put you out of mischief."

And for the rest of the afternoon Farmer Brown's boy was very busy around the edge of the Old Briar-patch.

XIX

Peter Rabbit and Danny Meadow Mouse Live High

PETER RABBIT sat in his secretest place in the dear Old Briar-patch with one of his long hind legs all swelled up and terribly sore because of the fine wire fast around it and cutting into it. He could hear Farmer Brown's boy going around on the edge of the dear Old Briar-patch and stopping every little while to do something. In spite of his pain, Peter was curious. Finally he called Danny Meadow Mouse.

"Danny, you are small and can keep out of sight easier than I can. Go as near as ever you dare to Farmer Brown's boy and find out what he is doing," said Peter Rabbit.

So Danny Meadow Mouse crept out as near to Farmer Brown's boy as ever he dared and studied and studied to make out what Farmer Brown's boy was doing. By and by he returned to Peter Rabbit.

"I don't know what he's doing, Peter, but he's putting something in every one of your private little paths leading in from the Green Meadows."

"Ha!" said Peter Rabbit.

"There are little loops of that queer stuff you've got hanging to your leg, Peter," continued Danny Meadow Mouse.

"Just so!" said Peter Rabbit.

"And he's put cabbage leaves and pieces of apple all around," said Danny.

"We must be careful!" said Peter Rabbit.

Peter's leg was in a very bad way, indeed, and Peter suffered a great deal of pain. The worst of it was, he didn't know how to get off the wire that was cutting into it so. He had tried to cut the wire with his big teeth, but he couldn't do it. Danny Meadow Mouse had tried and tried to gnaw the wire, but it wasn't of the least bit of use. But Danny wasn't easily discouraged, and he kept working and working at it. Once he thought he felt it slip a little. He said nothing, but kept right on working. Pretty soon he was sure that it slipped. He went right on working harder than ever. By and by he had it so loose that he slipped it right off of Peter's leg, and Peter didn't know anything about it. You see, that cruel wire snare had been so tight that Peter didn't have any feeling except of pain left in his leg, and so when Danny Meadow Mouse pulled the cruel wire snare off, Peter didn't know it until Danny held it up in front of him.

My, how thankful Peter was, and how he did thank Danny Meadow Mouse! But Danny said that it was nothing at all, just nothing at all, and that he owed more than that to Peter Rabbit for being so good to him and letting him live in the dear Old Briar-patch.

It was a long time before Peter could hop as he used to, but after the first day he managed to get around. He found that Farmer Brown's boy had spread those miserable wire snares in every one of his private little paths. But Peter knew what they were now. He showed Danny Meadow Mouse how he, because he was so small, could safely run about among the snares and steal all the cabbage leaves and apples which Farmer Brown's boy had put there for bait.

Danny Meadow Mouse thought this great fun and a great joke on Farmer Brown's boy. So every day he stole the bait, and he and Peter Rabbit lived high while Peter's leg was getting well. And all the time Farmer Brown's boy wondered and wondered why he couldn't catch Peter Rabbit.

XX

Timid Danny Meadow Mouse

DANNY MEADOW MOUSE is timid. Everybody says so, and what everybody says ought to be so. But just as anybody can make a mistake sometimes, so can everybody. Still, in this case, it is quite likely that everybody is right. Danny Meadow Mouse *is* timid. Ask Peter Rabbit. Ask Sammy Jay. Ask Striped Chipmunk. They will all tell you the same thing. Sammy Jay might even tell you that Danny is afraid of his own shadow, or that he tries to run away from his own tail. Of course this isn't true. Sammy Jay likes to say mean things. It isn't fair to Danny Meadow Mouse to believe what Sammy Jay says.

But the fact is Danny certainly is timid.

More than this, he isn't ashamed of it—not the least little bit.

"You see, it's this way," said Danny, as he sat on his door-step one sunny morning talking to his friend, old Mr. Toad. "If I weren't afraid, I wouldn't be all the time watching out, and if I weren't all the time watching out, I wouldn't have any more chance than that foolish red ant running across in front of you."

Old Mr. Toad looked where Danny was pointing, and his tongue darted out and back again so quickly that Danny wasn't sure that he saw it at all, but when he looked for the ant it was nowhere to be seen, and there was a satisfied twinkle in Mr. Toad's eyes. There was an answering twinkle in Danny's own eyes as he continued.

"No, Sir," said he, "I wouldn't stand a particle more chance than that foolish ant did. Now if I were big and strong, like Old Man Coyote, or had swift wings, like Skimmer the Swallow, or were so homely and ugly looking that no one wanted me, like—like—" Danny hesitated and then finished rather lamely, "like some folks I know, I suppose I wouldn't be afraid."

Old Mr. Toad looked up sharply when Danny mentioned homely and ugly looking people, but Danny was gazing far out across

the Green Meadows and looked so innocent
that Mr. Toad concluded that he couldn't have
had him in mind.

"Well," said he, thoughtfully scratching his
nose, "I suppose you may be right, but for my
part fear seems a very foolish thing. Now, I
don't know what it is. I mind my own business, and no one ever bothers me. I should
think it would be a very uncomfortable feeling."

"It is," replied Danny, "but, as I said before,
it is a very good thing to keep one on guard
when there are so many watching for one as
there are for me. Now there's Mr. Blacksnake
and—"

"Where?" exclaimed old Mr. Toad, turning
as pale as a Toad can turn, and looking uneas-
ily and anxiously in every direction.

Danny turned his head to hide a smile. If
old Mr. Toad wasn't showing fear, no one ever
did. "Oh," said he, "I didn't mean that he is
anywhere around here now. What I was going
to say was that there is Mr. Blacksnake and
Granny Fox and Reddy Fox and Redtail the
Hawk and Hooty the Owl and others I might
name, always watching for a chance to make
a dinner from poor little me. Do you wonder
that I am afraid most of the time?"

"No," replied old Mr. Toad. "No, I don't wonder that you are afraid. It must be dreadful to feel hungry eyes are watching for you every minute of the day and night, too."

"Oh, it's not so bad," replied Danny. "It's rather exciting. Besides, it keeps my wits sharp all the time. I am afraid I should find life very dull indeed if, like you, I feared nothing and nobody. By the way, see how queerly that grass is moving over there. It looks as if Mr. Blacksnake— Why, Mr. Toad, where are you going in such a hurry?"

"I've just remembered an important engagement with my cousin, Grandfather Frog, at the Smiling Pool," shouted old Mr. Toad over his shoulder, as he hurried so that he fell over his own feet.

Danny chuckled as he sat alone on his doorstep. "Oh, no, old Mr. Toad doesn't know what fear is!" said he. "Funny how some people won't admit what everybody can see for themselves. Now, I *am* afraid, and I'm willing to say so."

XXI

An Exciting Day for
Danny Meadow Mouse

DANNY MEADOW MOUSE started along one of his private little paths very early one morning. He was on his way to get a supply of a certain kind of grass-seed of which he is very fond. He had been thinking about that seed for some time and waiting for it to get ripe. Now it was just right, as he had found out the day before by a visit to the place where this particular grass grew. The only trouble was it grew a long way from Danny's home, and to reach it he had to cross an open place where the grass was so short that he couldn't make a path under it.

"I feel it in my bones that this is going to be an exciting day," said Danny to himself as he trotted along. "I suppose that if I were really wise, I would stay nearer home and do without that nice seed. But nothing is really worth having unless it is worth working for, and that seed will taste all the better if I have hard work getting it."

So he trotted along his private little path,

his ears wide open, and his eyes wide open, and his little nose carefully testing every Merry Little Breeze who happened along for any scent of danger which it might carry. Most of all he depended upon his ears, for the grass was so tall that he couldn't see over it, even when he sat up. He had gone only a little way when he thought he heard a queer rustling behind him. He stopped to listen. There it was again, and it certainly was right in the path behind him! He didn't need to be told who was making it. There was only one who could make such a sound as that—Mr. Blacksnake.

Now Danny can run very fast along his private little paths, but he knew that Mr. Blacksnake could run faster. "If my legs can't save me, my wits must," thought Danny as he started to run as fast as ever he could. "I must reach that fallen old hollow fence-post."

He was almost out of breath when he reached the post and scurried into the open end. He knew by the sound of the rustling that Mr. Blacksnake was right at his heels. Now the old post was hollow its whole length, but half-way there was an old knot-hole just big enough for Danny to squeeze through. Mr. Blacksnake didn't know anything about that hole, and because it was dark inside the old post, he didn't see Danny pop through it.

Danny ran back along the top of the log and was just in time to see the tip of Mr. Blacksnake's tail disappear inside. Then what do you think Danny did? Why, he followed Mr. Blacksnake right into the old post, but in doing it he didn't make the least little bit of noise.

Mr. Blacksnake kept right on through the old post and out the other end, for he was sure that that was the way Danny had gone. He kept right on along the little path. Now Danny knew that he wouldn't go very far before he found out that he had been fooled, and of course he would come back. So Danny waited only long enough to get his breath and then ran back along the path to where another little path branched off. For just a minute he paused.

"If Mr. Blacksnake follows me, he will be sure to think that of course I have taken this other little path," thought Danny, "so I won't do it."

Then he ran harder than ever, until he came to a place where two little paths branched off, one to the right and one to the left. He took the latter and scampered on, sure that by this time Mr. Blacksnake would be so badly fooled that he would give up the chase. And Danny was right.

"Brains are better far than speed
As wise men long ago agreed,"

said Danny, as he trotted on his way for the grass-seed he liked so well. "I felt it in my bones that this would be an exciting day. I wonder what next."

XXII

What Happened Next to Danny Meadow Mouse

DANNY IS SO USED to narrow escapes that he doesn't waste any time thinking about them. He didn't this time. "He who tries to look two ways at once is pretty sure to see nothing," says Danny, and he knew that if he thought too much about the things that had already happened, he couldn't keep a sharp watch for the things that might happen.

Nothing more happened as he hurried along his private little path to the edge of a great patch of grass so short that he couldn't hide under it. He had got to cross this, and all the way he would be in plain sight of any one who happened to be near. Very cautiously he peeped out and looked this way and looked that way, not forgetting to look up in the sky. He could see no one anywhere. Drawing a long breath, Danny started across the open place as fast as his short legs could take him.

Now all the time, Redtail the Hawk had been sitting in a tree some distance away, sitting so still that he looked like a part of the tree itself. That is why Danny hadn't seen him. But Redtail saw Danny the instant he started across the open place, for Redtail's eyes are very keen, and he can see a great distance. With a satisfied chuckle, he spread his broad wings and started after Danny.

Just about half-way to the safety of the long grass on the other side, Danny gave a hurried look behind him, and his heart seemed to jump right into his mouth, for there was Redtail with his cruel claws already set to seize him! Danny gave a frightened squeak, for he thought that surely this time he would be caught. But he didn't mean to give up without trying to escape. Three jumps ahead of him was a queer looking thing. He didn't know what it was, but if there was a hole in it he might yet fool Redtail.

One jump! Would he be able to reach it? Two jumps! There *was* a hole in it! Three

With another frightened squeak, Danny dived
into the opening just in time. *Page 73.*

jumps! With another frightened squeak, Danny dived into the opening just in time. And what do you think he was in? Why, an old tomato can Farmer Brown's boy had once used to carry bait in when he went fishing at the Smiling Pool. He had dropped it there on his way home.

Redtail screamed with rage and disappointment as he struck the old can with his great claws. He had been sure, very sure of Danny Meadow Mouse this time! He tried to pick the can up, but he couldn't get hold of it. It just rolled away from him every time, try as he would. Finally, in disgust, he gave up and flew back to the tree from which he had first seen Danny.

Of course Danny had been terribly frightened when the can rolled, and by the noise the claws of Redtail made when they struck his queer hiding-place. But he wisely decided that the best thing he could do was to stay there for a while. And it was very fortunate that he did so, as he was very soon to find out.

XXIII

Reddy Fox Grows Curious

DANNY MEADOW MOUSE had sat perfectly still for a long time inside the old tomato can in which he had found a refuge from Redtail the Hawk. He didn't dare so much as put his head out for a look around, lest Redtail should be circling overhead ready to pounce on him.

"If I stay here long enough, he'll get tired and go away, if he hasn't already," thought Danny. "This has been a pretty exciting morning so far, and I find that I am a little tired. I may as well take a nap while I am waiting to make sure that the way is clear."

With that Danny curled up in the old tomato can. But it wasn't meant that Danny should have that nap. He had closed his eyes, but his ears were still open, and presently he heard soft footsteps drawing near. His eyes flew open, and he forgot all about sleep, you may be sure, for those footsteps sounded familiar. They sounded to Danny very, very much like the footsteps of—whom do you think? Why, Reddy Fox! Danny's heart began to beat faster as he listened. Could it be? He didn't dare peep out. Presently a little whiff of scent blew into the old tomato can. Then Danny knew—it *was* Reddy Fox.

"Oh, dear! I hope he doesn't find that I am in here!" thought Danny. "I wonder what under the sun has brought him up here just now."

If the truth were to be known, it was curiosity that had brought Reddy up there. Reddy had been hunting for his breakfast some distance away on the Green Meadows when Redtail the Hawk had tried so hard to catch Danny Meadow Mouse. Reddy's sharp eyes had seen Redtail the minute he left the tree in pursuit of Danny, and he had known by the way Redtail flew that he saw something he wanted to catch. He had watched Redtail swoop down and had heard his scream of rage when he missed Danny because Danny had dodged into the old tomato can. He had seen Redtail strike and strike again at something on the ground, and finally fly off in disgust with empty claws.

"Now, I wonder what it was Redtail was after and why he didn't get it," thought Reddy. "He acts terribly put out and disappointed. I believe I'll go over there and find out."

Off he started at a smart trot towards the

patch of short grass where he had seen Redtail the Hawk striking at something on the
ground. As he drew near, he crept very softly
until he reached the very edge of the open
patch. There he stopped and looked sharply
all over it. There was nothing to be seen but
an old tomato can. Reddy had seen it many
times before.

"Now what under the sun could Redtail
have been after here?" thought Reddy. "The
grass isn't long enough for a grasshopper to
hide in, and yet Redtail didn't get what he
was after. It's very queer. It certainly is very
queer."

He trotted out and began to run back and
forth with his nose to the ground, hoping that
his nose would tell him what his eyes
couldn't. Back and forth, back and forth he
ran, and then suddenly he stopped.

"Ha!" exclaimed Reddy. He had found the
scent left by Danny Meadow Mouse when he
ran across towards the old tomato can. Right
up to the old can Reddy's nose led him. He
hopped over the old can, but on the other side
he could find no scent of Danny Meadow
Mouse. In a flash he understood, and a gleam
of satisfaction shone in his yellow eyes as he
turned back to the old can. He knew that
Danny must be hiding in there.

"I've got you this time!" he snarled, as he sniffed at the opening in the end of the can.

XXIV

Reddy Fox Loses His Temper

REDDY FOX had caught Danny Meadow Mouse, and yet he hadn't caught him. He had found Danny hiding in the old tomato can, and it didn't enter Reddy's head that he couldn't get Danny out when he wanted to. He was in no hurry. He had had a pretty good breakfast of grasshoppers, and so he thought he would torment Danny a while before gobbling him up. He lay down so that he could peep in at the open end of the old can and see Danny trying to make himself as small as possible at the other end. Reddy grinned until he showed all his long teeth. Reddy always is a bully, especially when his victim is a great deal smaller and weaker than himself.

"I've got you this time, Mr. Smarty, haven't I?" taunted Reddy.

Danny didn't say anything.

"You think you've been very clever because

you have fooled me two or three times, don't you? Well, this time I've got you where your tricks won't work," continued Reddy, "so what are you going to do about it?"

Danny didn't answer. The fact is, he was too frightened to answer. Besides, he didn't know what he could do. So he just kept still, but his bright eyes never once left Reddy's cruel face. For all his fright, Danny was doing some hard thinking. He had been in tight places before and had learned never to give up hope. Something might happen to frighten Reddy away. Anyway, Reddy had got to get him out of that old can before he would admit that he was really caught.

For a long time Reddy lay there licking his chops and saying all the things he could think of to frighten poor Danny Meadow Mouse. At last he grew tired of this and made up his mind that it was time to end it and Danny Meadow Mouse at the same time. He thrust his sharp nose in at the opening in the end of the old can, but the opening was too small for him to get more than his nose in, and he only scratched it on the sharp edges without so much as touching Danny.

"I'll pull you out," said Reddy and thrust in one black paw.

Danny promptly bit it so hard that Reddy yelped with pain and pulled it out in a hurry. Presently he tried again with the other paw. Danny bit this one harder still, and Reddy danced with pain and anger. Then he lost his temper completely, a very foolish thing to do, as it always is. He hit the old can, and away it rolled with Danny Meadow Mouse inside. This seemed to make Reddy angrier than ever. He sprang after it and hit it again. Then he batted it first this way and then that way, growing angrier and angrier. And all the time Danny Meadow Mouse managed to keep inside, although he got a terrible shaking up.

Back and forth across the patch of short grass Reddy knocked the old can, and he was in such a rage that he didn't notice where he was knocking it to. Finally he sent it spinning into the long grass on the far side of the open patch, close to one of Danny's private little paths. Like a flash Danny was out and scurrying along the little path. He dodged into another and presently into a third, which brought him to a tangle of barbed wire left there by Farmer Brown when he had built a new fence. Under this he was safe.

"Phew!" exclaimed Danny, breathing very hard. "That was the narrowest escape yet! But

I guess I'll get that special grass-seed I started out for, after all."

And he did, while to this day Reddy Fox wonders how Danny got out of the old tomato can without him knowing it.

> And so you see what temper does
> For those who give it rein;
> It cheats them of the very thing
> They seek so hard to gain.

Danny has had many more adventures, but there isn't room to tell about them here. Besides Grandfather Frog is anxious that you should hear about the queer things that have happened to him. They are told in the next book.*

THE END.

*NOTE: *The Adventures of Grandfather Frog* is available from Dover Publications (0-486-27400-4).

✧DOVER✧
CHILDREN'S THRIFT CLASSICS

All books complete and unabridged, except where noted.
96pp., 5³/₁₆″ × 8¼″, paperbound.